# AND YOU THINK YOUR JOB STINKS

# AND YOU THINK YOUR JOB STINKS

## Everyone Has a Hang-in-there Day

Karla O'Malley

authorHOUSE®

AuthorHouse™ LLC
1663 Liberty Drive
Bloomington, IN 47403
www.authorhouse.com
Phone: 1-800-839-8640

Published by AuthorHouse   08/09/2013

ISBN: 978-1-4817-6307-3 (sc)
ISBN: 978-1-4817-6306-6 (e)

Library of Congress Control Number: 2013910951

Any people depicted in stock imagery provided by Thinkstock are models, and such images are being used for illustrative purposes only.
Certain stock imagery © Thinkstock.

This book is printed on acid-free paper.

Because of the dynamic nature of the Internet, any web addresses or links contained in this book may have changed since publication and may no longer be valid. The views expressed in this work are solely those of the author and do not necessarily reflect the views of the publisher, and the publisher hereby disclaims any responsibility for them.

# CONTENTS

# FOREWORD

If you are currently thinking that you have the worst job in the world, and nobody should have to put up with all you do, this book is for you. The stories in this book are based on real-life experiences. Some are eyebrow-raising, some are knee-slapping funny, and some are simply reminding us that we are all human. The average American spends over 2,000 hours a year at work. Finding a happy balance, and learning to deal with the frustrations, is of utmost importance.

To quote a very intelligent man, my husband, "Everyone has a hang-in-there day at work." He said this to me after I had broken down from all the frustrations of my job. I loved the work; I was improving processes and helping people. The frustrations came from the human element. I was working with some very unreasonable, untrustworthy, and immoral people. I was ready to quit. There had been so many unbelievable events occurring around the office that I honestly looked around for someone filming us for a reality television show. When I would come home from work and watch *The Office* on NBC, I felt as if I was working overtime. My boss was a master at making people even more uncomfortable than the show's Michael Scott character. On television the discomfort was funny, but it was not welcome in real life. Having spent more than 20 years in Human Resources, I had learned to hold my opinions to myself, to try to see every side of a situation, and to remember that everything I said or did could end up replayed in a courtroom. I had the feeling that nobody had ever had to put up with as many idiotic schemes as I did.

At first my frustrations really got to me. I lost sleep, and did not have much of an appetite. I grew numb to my frustrations, and started simply living on autopilot. Finally I started to be amused by my frustrations, considering them entertainment. After all, who would expect an executive vice-president to show up for an interview intoxicated? Who would expect an officer of a company to use his company credit card at a strip club? Who would expect a janitor to throw away legal documents needed for a wrongful-termination lawsuit?

After my husband reminded me that everybody had hang-in-there days, I thought that he just may be right. Maybe I wasn't the only one who was miserable with her job. Maybe there were other people who had aches in the pit of their stomachs every morning when they walked through their office doors. There are bad bosses and awful co-workers everywhere, hanging around every water cooler, and sitting in every conference room. Maybe there really were rats in the rat race!

If you are thinking of quitting your job because of the human element involved, you may change your mind after reading this book. You are not alone in feeling the frustrations of work. Millions go to work with that painful pit in their stomachs. Every day an executive of a company somewhere reminds us they are still human. Rarely do you find someone who truly enjoys his job. Everyone experiences hang-in-there days at some points in their careers.

Enjoy life and see the humor in it!
~ Joy Dye

(The stories in this book are based on real life experiences. The names, locations and companies have been changed as to not embarrass anybody involved in the story. If you recognize yourself or a co-worker in these stories, it could simply be coincidence—*or is it?*)

# THE LAYOFF . . . NOT

## "Angry? No I'm not angry you took a job elsewhere."

Doyle was arrogant, naïve, and stupidly lucky. He was the Executive Vice President of a small company in Kansas, but was definitely in over his head. He lacked the common sense God gave a goose. All of his decisions in life had been focused on how the outcome would benefit him personally. Never once did he give to charity, or hold the door open for a stranger. He was in his mid-fifties, but tried to fit in the skin of a 25-year-old. He would hang out in bars where the patrons were the same age as his children. He thought he fit right in, but the other bar patrons thought he was a little old and moldy. Not wanting to be rude, the young crowd went along with Doyle's warped perception of himself. This only encouraged Doyle to continue making a fool of himself every Saturday night at the bars on River Walk Boulevard.

In Doyle's younger days he had gotten his GED, and started his career as a taxi driver. By the time he was 22 Doyle had become one of New York City's finest cabbies. But after a few years of driving a taxi he had had enough of pine-tree air fresheners and 15-minute small talk conversations with his passengers. He started dreaming of grandeur. Like many young men, he wanted to run his own company. The one thing that separated Doyle from most every other person in his situation was that he decided to do something about it. Doyle made contact with a wealthy man who was looking for a business opportunity. If nothing else, Doyle was quite a talker, and could win someone's friendship, if just for the evening. He was able to sell the wealthy man on his idea for a limousine rental company, and the rest was history. At the age of 25, Doyle became the Executive Vice President of *Doyle's Limo Service*. He was able to grow the company through luck, a little skill, and an Artesian well of cash from his wealthy investor friend.

Doyle's success with his limo company only fueled his ego and attitude. His presence in the office was repulsive, but if you wanted to keep your job, you had to talk to him respectfully. Massaging his ego was the only way to get along with him. The employees' real opinion of Doyle was left for the time of exhale in the privacy of their own homes.

Things around Doyle's company were starting to show the effects of the bad economy. Limousines are not something that people often rent when the unemployment rate is near double-digits. Rumors were starting to run rapidly around the small office. How could their company continue to be successful? Everyone was starting to consider what other jobs they might apply for if the company closed. But the endless supply of money from the wealthy investor was not information that Doyle shared with his employees. No, sir! If he shared the fact that they had a fountain of wealth supporting them, Doyle would not appear to be the genius businessman that he had everyone believing he was.

Kim had worked hard for Doyle over the years. It was well known that Doyle did not give raises very often. The more money he gave in raises, the less money he would have for himself. Giving Kim a raise might just stop the rumors about financial worries. He knew his employees talked.

In fact, his 20 employees did not keep secrets from each other. News of Kim's raise would get around quickly. This would put an ease to their worries and their concerns about finding employment elsewhere.

Doyle decided to meet with Kim to discuss her raise, but not without a little personal fun in the process. Doyle called Kim into his office. He started with the statement, "Kim, you know that things have not been real good around here lately." Kim started to worry that this conversation was not going to be a good one. Doyle then said, "I am sure you know what a bad economy we are in right now, and that companies have to cut back everywhere." Kim thought this is it. I am going to be fired. Kim's eyes started to tear up. Doyle continued. "I have been considering all options for my company, and I have had to make some hard decisions." Kim started to cry. Doyle then said "Oh stop it; I am giving you a raise, stupid!"

Pay raise or not, Kim started looking for another job as soon as she got home that night.

~~~~~~~~~~~~~~~~~~~~~~~~~~~~~~~~~~~~~~~~~~~~~~~

"The only way you're going to grow is to be in difficult situations."
~ Mike Krzyzewski

"A joke is a hard poke if the timing is not right."
~ Joy Dye

# PICK A CARD—ANY CARD

"Did you see a cocktail napkin
with our entire marketing campaign on it?"

Dean was Assistant to the Vice-President of Administration for a jewelry company. His title came with a company car, vacation time when he saw fit, membership at a local country club, and a company credit card. Life was good. He worked hard to get to this position, and felt entitled to the perks. He had paid his own college expenses with a part-time job and scholarships. He gave up the weekends of partying with his friends so his strong grades would earn a reoccurring scholarship, and he did not allow himself to date while going to college—girls were expensive and time consuming. If any of his college friends needed a study buddy, they could count on finding Dean at the library. Yes, Dean had sacrificed a lot to get to the position he held.

Dean's cherrywood desk was neat and orderly. His calendar pictured a waterfall scene from Hawaii, and a red circle around the upcoming weekend. That weekend was the one in which Dean and his friends from college would make their annual trip to a distant city, where they would cut loose and recharge. No wives, no girlfriends, and no cell phones were allowed on their trips. They had not missed a single annual excursion since they graduated from SMSU. Jobs and girlfriends would come and go, but this annual trip was solid. This year the guys had planned a trip to St. Louis. They would take in a Cardinals' baseball game, check out the Arch, and eat a little Italian food on "The Hill".

Their seats for the Cardinals' game were not spectacular, but they were among an amusing crowd. Foul ball territory, cold beer, and close enough to one of the outfielders to offer their opinions of how the game was going. Dean was sure their opinions were very useful and appreciated by the outfielder. He could swear he even saw the leftfielder crack a smile at some of their comments, comments like, "Hey Dracula, wake up your bat!" and, "You couldn't even throw a party!" But Dean's all-time favorite was "Hey Ump, is this your cell phone? Because it has three missed calls!" The game went into extra innings and extra beers. The Cardinals won in the 11th inning with a home run to left field.

The trip up the Arch called for yet more beer. After all, they had to work up the nerve to ride what Dean called "an egg" to the top of the Arch. The "egg" was an oval shaped cart that lifted visitors to the top of the Arch in a Ferris wheel fashion. It was roomy, safe, and built to smoothly fit inside the interior walls of the arch-shaped tunnel. For anyone afraid of heights the trip to the top was a heart-pounding experience. Once there, more "liquid courage" would be required to work up the nerve to ride the egg back down. Alcohol was not allowed inside the arch, but that did not stop the guys from sneaking a flask of Jack in their jackets. They had become experts at finding ways around authority. They forgot about eating on The Hill, but did not forget to order a few more rounds at a local bar.

The trip was fun, although not eventful. Nobody ended up in jail, like on their trip to Las Vegas in 2009, or missed their flight back home, like on their trip to Denver in 2011. They enjoyed a quick, noisy, fun-filled weekend, and then back to the office and reality on Monday.

Back at the office things were routine. Dean got back to his networking with customers and vendors, and working with his direct reports on improving the company's processes. Everything continued as normal for a week or so. Then everything screeched to a halt when Dean got his charge card statement from accounting. There was a charge for $532.54 to HCV in St. Louis, MO. Dean had no idea what HCV was, and what he could have possibly purchased for $532.54?

Dean's first thought was that someone else had somehow gotten information off his credit card and made this purchase. He started his research. To start tracking down the culprit who made these charges with his company card he got a phone number for HCV and called to determine the nature of their business. When Dean placed the call he found that HCV was a strip club. Then the memories started coming back. While the trip to St. Louis was uneventful, he did remember something about going to a strip club. He must have had a little too much to drink, spent a little too much money, and did not notice which card he used while there.

Dean slowly made the walk of shame to the Accounting Department to write his company a check for $532.54.

~~~~~~~~~~~~~~~~~~~~~~~~~~~~~~~~~~~~~~~~~~~

"God watches over drunks and third baseman."
~ Leo Durocher

"If you make a mistake—own it, fix it and move on."
~ Joy Dye

# WHERE'S JOHN

"Then I made the mistake of telling my employees that if they didn't like the way I ran the company they could sue me."

As John pulled into his driveway after work he felt relieved to be home. An accident on the highway had made traffic particularly heavy. Repeatedly pushing on the gas, and then the brake, was not an exercise his 60-year-old ankle enjoyed. Holding his foot in a ready-to-brake position was a nuisance, but he was bothered more by thoughts of the people involved in the accident. He could not help but wonder about them. Were they okay? The roads were dry and the weather clear; what could have possibly caused an accident on such a beautiful day? As he drove by the site of the accident he was glad to see that it was just a little fender-bender. No ambulance needed, just a wrecker to haul off the injured cars.

On his way up the sidewalk to his front door John admired the vibrantly-colored knockout roses. His wife Joanne nurtured the roses as carefully as she had their own children when they were young. The roses seemed to help fill that empty-nest pain. It had been very hard to watch their two children grow up and leave home. John missed coaching his sons' baseball teams. All the practices, games, and tournaments took a lot of time, but it had been time well spent. Their sons were successful in their careers, marriages, and friendships. John liked to think that the time he spent with them helped ensure their successes. Yes, John missed having his boys at home, and had filled the hole in his heart by teaching tricks to Otis, their pet bulldog.

Joanne had turned her emptiness into becoming the neighborhood botanist. Neighbors often asked her how she was able to grow her roses so healthy. Joanne would simply smile and say, "Lots of sunshine and water." John knew her secret—it was dried banana peels! Since Joanne had discovered that roses love banana peels, John had never had so many banana dishes. He loved bananas, but preferred them straight out of the peel, not mashed and spiced. Joanne experimented in the kitchen, and had come up with such dishes as banana and brown sugar pancakes, banana chocolate chip muffins, banana peanut butter cheesecake, and her favorite snack, fried banana slices.

The roses gave their house a wonderful curb appeal, and the aroma was welcoming for the stroll to the front door. John opened the front door with his usual, "Honey, I'm home!" As John bent down to pet their overly excited bulldog, he felt a returning tightness in his chest. He had been feeling a reoccurring tightness since noon. He had gone to a nearby steakhouse for lunch with the guys from the factory. He had passed off the uncomfortable tightness in his chest as the result of overeating yet again. Overeating had become a habit, and the size of his belly was evidence of that. The guys from work said he had "Dunlap disease". When he asked what Dunlap disease was, they laughed and said, "Your belly has done lapped over your belt." The guys were always cracking jokes like that. Working on the line at the plant got boring, and John appreciated their humor. John had worked at the plant for 15 years, and had developed some close friendships. Just five more years and retirement would be a reality.

Tonight John thought that an aspirin and some needed rest would take care of the chest pain. After a hard day at work he was looking forward to some downtime. John's work was not easy. He worked the slicer at a box manufacturer. One careless move, one glance away from the slicer, and he could cut a finger right off. There was talk about automating his job. This concerned John, but being so close to retirement he tried not to let it get to him.

The plant had gone 424 days in a row without a workplace accident. One would think they would at least get a pat on the back for a record like that, but not from their boss, Mr. Kline. It seemed Mr. Kline got pleasure out of ordering people around. He would reprimand a member of his staff in front of everybody, not caring what embarrassment he might cause. Nobody would dare be late on Mr. Kline's shift, not even five minutes. He would make late employees pay by putting them on the worst detail jobs he could find. John always felt a little sorry for him. Only a person who was miserable inside would want to be so abrasive to other people. Mr. Kline was a very demanding man who had a permanent frown plastered on his face. Yes sir, a day under Mr. Kline's dictatorship made John look forward to a quiet evening at home with Joanne. He would feel more like himself in the morning.

After a light dinner of tuna salad and banana bread, John and Joanne snuggled up on the couch to watch television. *The Big Bang Theory* was on, and they really liked that show. Seems there weren't very many good shows on these days, but CBS had hit the mark with this one. John and Joanne had turned into dedicated viewers. Halfway during the episode, Joanne noticed that John had a pained look in his face and was not breathing normally. Joanne wasted no time. She had been noticing John's lack of energy lately, and knew he was a prime candidate for a heart attack. She called 9-1-1. The paramedics reached their house within minutes and whisked John away to the hospital.

John did not show up for work the next day. It was Friday, and John never missed work unexpectedly. Besides, Friday was the day the guys went for a Mexican food lunch at *Mi'Casa*. John loved Mexican food, especially the stuffed jalapeños, which were as yummy as they were caloricious. The day went on as normal. Some of John's co-workers noticed that John was not at his station on the line, but their boss had a temporary worker filling his spot, so they figured John had called in sick. John's friends missed him at lunch at *Mi'Casa*. They remarked that it was unusual for him to be sick. Tim even mentioned stopping by John's house on his way home that night, just to make sure everything was okay. The afternoon dragged by. The workers on the floor of the plant couldn't help but watch the clock. It seemed that clocks at work moved slower than clocks at home. Their work was hard and tedious. Five o'clock could not come too soon.

At 4:59 PM the box-making machines automatically shut down. A sense of relief was felt across the factory floor, and the workers almost immediately removed their protective goggles and gloves. Some workers had conversations of meeting for a quick drink before going home, while others were planning on heading to the high school baseball field to watch their beloved home team play their final baseball game of the season. Then Mr. Kline's voice came over the intercom. "Your attention, please. I regret to inform you that John Adams passed away last night. Our condolences to his family."

You see, Mr. Kline had learned of John's death at 8:00 AM that morning, but he did not inform his staff of John's passing before quitting time. He knew how much John was liked, and the effect news of his death would have on the productivity of the floor. He wanted to get a full day's worth of work out of the workers before all the feelings of sadness, the anger, and the reminiscing started. He figured they would have the weekend to get over it, and be ready for another full day of work on Monday.

~~~~~~~~~~~~~~~~~~~~~~~~~~~~~~~~~~~~~~~~~~~~~~~~

"If I have the gift of prophecy and can fathom all mysteries and all knowledge, and if I have a faith that can move mountains, but have not love, I am nothing."
~ I Corinthians 13:2

"Be the boss you have always wanted, and you will have the staff you have always wanted."
~ Joy Dye

# WASH YOUR HANDS, PLEASE

*"According to my sources, you spent 12 minutes in the bathroom. Your pay will be docked accordingly."*

Jennifer was a recruiter for a trucking company in Wisconsin. She worked hard at finding quality drivers. With the recent slowdown in the transportation industry, safe drivers with a stable work history had become more and more rare. She used all the marketing options she could think of—websites, local papers, and online social networks. You name it; she had tried it. The trick with truck drivers was to find where they go when they are looking for work. With such a diverse group of professionals she had to be creative. Some drivers were accustomed to using the computer to find employment, while others relied solely on CB chatter to get the skinny on what companies were good to work for and what companies to avoid. Jennifer's hard work paid off, for her company seldom had an empty truck.

Everyday Jennifer came to the office her voicemail would be full of messages from drivers wanting to talk about job openings. She would promptly call them back. Some of the drivers turned out to be wonderful additions to the company, while others would have to be politely sent on their way. She made a point to call every driver back. Phone calls and e-mails that did not get a requested response were Jennifer's pet peeve. If someone took the time to call or send an e-mail, then the recipient should take the time to respond, she thought.

One otherwise typical Monday Jennifer arrived at the office, greeting everyone with her normal cheery smile. After getting a cup of coffee and checking the supply of paper in the copy machine, she sat down at her desk, got out her notepad, and was prepared to take notes on the 23 messages left on her phone over the weekend. No doubt all 23 messages were responses from her recent posting on a local job board.

On the ninth message Jennifer wrote down the name the driver had given and patiently waited for the voice on the recording to give her his phone number. As she listened the driver went on about his work history and his safe driving record. He then said ". . . so call me back. I would like to know more about the truck driving job." Jennifer thought she heard a small trickle of water in the background the entire time caller number nine was leaving his message. She then heard a toilet flush. Oh my goodness . . . did that driver leave the message asking about employment while he was relieving himself?

Needless to say, this driver did not get a call-back. Jennifer also felt compelled to disinfect her phone.

~~~~~~~~~~~~~~~~~~~~~~~~~~~~~~~~~~~~~~~~~~~~~~

"Without feelings of respect, what is there to distinguish
men from beasts?"
~ Confucius

"Not every voice mail or email deserves a reply."
~ Joy Dye

# YOU CAN LEAD A HORSE TO WATER

## "Don't be upset if I ignore your advice."

Robin had worked in Corporate Development for years. She was a veteran at training people on how to source applicants, how to interview and retain top performers, and how to understand Workman's Compensation, FMLA, and Corrective Action Policies. She had spent many hours on the other side of the table negotiating health care premiums for her company. Being so good at her job had made her well known, and she was frequently asked to present at seminars. She had even authored a few books on the subject of hiring and retaining top talent.

She found that her job was taking away from her family time. Her children were growing up very fast, and the 60-hour weeks were getting to be just too much. She had already missed too many softball games when her daughter was pitching, and too many soccer goals scored by her son. Robin wanted to slow down a little. She thought that going to work for a smaller company would provide an easier, calmer atmosphere. She answered an advertisement from a small construction company that was looking for someone to be their Office Manager. The ad had some misspellings and poor grammar. Robin thought that this company could use some professionalism, and she was just the person to provide it.

One week after Robin responded to the ad, the construction company called her for an interview. She was to meet at their office at 2:00 PM on Wednesday. Robin had some vacation time that she was going to otherwise lose, so she requested the day off. Dressed in her pleated skirt and silk shirt, she pulled up to the front of *Made Right Construction*. She did not want to be dressed too professionally, as she could tell that this company had more of a homespun atmosphere. Her skirt and blouse would give just enough of a professional presence, without being pretentious.

When Robin arrived at the office she was greeted by Donna, the office secretary. The owners were out of town at a golf tournament and they had put Donna in charge of the interview and hiring decision. Donna said, "I am not really sure what I am supposed to be asking you for this interview. I guess you have the experience we need and we'll give it a shot. When can you start?" Robin was a little taken aback at this question-less interview, but the more she was around this company, the more she thought they could use her help. It was an awkward interview, but she was already brainstorming on ideas to help this company flourish. The pay was a little less than she was currently making, but for a less stressful position and more time to spend with her family, it was well worth the loss in income.

Two gentlemen, Jim and Bryan, owned the company. After being with the company for only a week Robin's enthusiasm was diminishing. Jim and Bryan were so blunt and raw that she was starting to feel out of place. Robin referred to Jim and Bryan as Stumb and

Dupid in her mind. They were very rough around the edges, and did not have a professional hair on their heads. Being their Office Manager was going to be a challenge. Robin had come from a refined, professional atmosphere; a place where people showed up before 8:00 AM and left after 5:00 PM; a place where men wore ties and acted like gentlemen; a place where women wore dresses or pantsuits, and sat with their ankles crossed. At this construction company things were different. Dispatchers wore shorts and flip-flops. It was unusual for anyone to show up before 8:00 AM, and by 4:30 PM the office was so empty you could hear the lonely ring of the phones echo down the hallway. Yes, this atmosphere would be a challenge.

At Jim's request Robin sat in with him on an interview. He scheduled an appointment to interview a candidate for their electrical team. She was told to simply observe, so that she would understand how Jim and Bryan wanted their interviews to be conducted. They wanted a calm, easy-going atmosphere, where they could really get to know the candidates. Jim wanted Robin to see how he did it. He wanted her to understand what he was looking for in his employees. The applicant showed up at the office five minutes early. Jim welcomed him with a handshake. The three of them then walked into the conference room. Jim introduced Robin, asked the applicant to take a seat, and then started right in with his list of rapid-fire questions. Robin sat there with pen and paper in hand and quietly listened. Jim asked questions like, "Are you married? Do you have kids?" and the most jaw dropping of all, "Do you like to party after work?" When the interview was over Robin was sure there was a 50-pound weight on her jaw, because she had a very hard time keeping her mouth shut.

Robin thought she would have to gently direct Jim and Bryan on appropriate interview questions, on and why some questions could lead to legal issues. She found a simple summary on this topic, and some case studies that had ended badly in court. Robin forwarded a report to Jim and Bryan in an e-mail, with a very carefully worded lead in. She did not want to insult them, but definitely had to help them, and protect the company from potential legal action.

They had posted an advertisement for a secretarial position. After carefully evaluating the applicant pool, Robin narrowed her choices down to the three people she would call in for an interview. Jim, Bryan, and Robin discussed the format of the interviews. Robin gave Jim and Bryan a list of approved questions to ask. The men liked the questions and agreed to the plan. They would take turns asking the questions. If someone wanted to dig deeper into the candidate's response, that was fine, as long as they stayed on topic. One of the applicant's interviews was scheduled for 3:30 that afternoon. Bryan was late, so Jim and Robin made small talk with the candidate waiting for Bryan's arrival. The small talk made Robin a little nervous. She wondered how Jim would do without a script. Robin was pleased that Jim had remained professional during their chat. She thought that maybe Jim understood and appreciated the report she had sent him. Bryan arrived at 3:45. He apologized, introduced himself to the applicant, and they started in with the official interview questions. The interview got off to a good start. Robin asked the lead question. "Tell us about your work history, and how your experience would apply to this position." The candidate responded appropriately. Then Bryan started in with his questions. "Why would you like to work for us?" "What are your future plans for your career?" Robin thought this was a good sign. Her e-mail had worked, and that Bryan understood what she tried to convey to them, and the seriousness of inappropriate interview questions. Then Jim started asking his questions. "You are not wearing a ring. Are you dating anyone?" This was followed by, "What church do you go to?" Then he looked to Robin and said "Oops! I am not supposed to ask those questions, am I?" Robin quickly redirected the conversation with another question, hoping the candidate did not realize what had just taken place.

Robin soon went back to working at a place with a refined, professional atmosphere, a place where people showed up before 8:00 AM and left after 5:00 PM, a place where men wore ties and acted like gentlemen, a place where women wore dresses and pantsuits, and sat with their ankles crossed. Yes, she went back to a place where the horse is smart enough to take a drink when it gets led to the water.

~~~~~~~~~~~~~~~~~~~~~~~~~~~~~~~~~~~~~~~~~~~~~~~~~~

"A word to the wise ain't necessary—it's the stupid ones that
need the advice."
~ Bill Cosby

"I learned long ago, never to wrestle with a pig. You get
dirty, and besides, the pig likes it."
~ George Bernard Shaw

# A DEAD END JOB

# "Whoever is hired they will be fast on their feet."

Paul was a mechanic for a car repair shop in Minneapolis. He would always take the newspaper with him on his lunch break. He would skip through the headlines, comics and advertisements and go straight to the obituaries. His co-worker Alvin thought that this was peculiar, but did not pay very much attention to it. He figured Paul just a little bit strange.

One day while Paul was on his way back to the lunchroom with the newspaper in his hand, Alvin could not help himself. He stopped Paul and asked him why he always went straight to the obituaries when he read the paper. Paul smiled and said, "I am looking for job openings."

~~~~~~~~~~~~~~~~~~~~~~~~~~~~~~~~~~~~~~~~~~~~~~~~~

"Choose a job you love, and you will never have to work a
day in your life."
~ Confucius

"Happiness is an inside job."
~ William Arthur Ward

## "Happy Hour is rough on the 'get up at 4 am' crowd."

It was the Friday before a greatly anticipated July 4th weekend. Karen had been the Human Resources Director for a small golf supply company for four years. In the short time that she had been in her position she had managed to resolve several employee-relation issues, rebuild their healthcare insurance to a more robust plan, and rewrite their handbook so that it was solid and court-battlefield proof. She did all this while also saving the company money by revamping her departmental budget. She had done an exceptional job for the company, but still took frustrations home with her sometimes. Yes, Karen did let work get to her more than she should, but when an employee is as dedicated as Karen it is hard not to let things get personal. Her work was her baby, and she defended it, nurtured it, and thought about it like she would her own child. Sometimes the frustrations would invade her dreams, and she would toss and turn through the night while the rest of the world slept. She was okay with this, but she knew that her restlessness was also affecting her husband's sleep. It was hard for him to sleep with a constant blanket pulling, bed rippling, heavily sighing, tossing, turning wife beside him.

The two owners of the company, Dennis and Terry, were a lot like the "jocks" Karen knew in high school. They were fun loving, had head-turning good looks, and liked to party. Strike that, LOVED to party. When they had to get serious they could, but they were both very uncomfortable, and about as graceful as hogs on ice, in a conference room.

Terry had scheduled a second interview with a candidate for a sales position for 3:00 PM on Friday, July 2nd. The candidate's name was Bruce. Karen was to meet Terry and Bruce at a local sports bar. Karen thought that it was unusual to schedule an interview so close to the start of a holiday, especially for her party-hound boss. But, like always, she did as she was told without question.

Karen had not seen Terry all day. She knew they had to get to the sports bar for the interview, and was concerned that Terry may have forgotten about it. It was not unusual for Terry to just blow off the Friday before a holiday, but this interview was pretty important, and after all, *he* was the one who had scheduled it. She waited as long as she could for him to arrive at the office. Finally, she sent a text to Terry at 2:45. "Terry—I am on my way to the interview. If you cannot make it, I will handle it and fill you in. Otherwise, I will see you at 3:00." Karen left the office and drove to the sports bar.

When Karen got there, she saw Bruce sitting at a table with his hand cupped in front of his mouth. He was blowing into his hand, checking his breath. Karen thought this was cute and boyish. She could tell she liked this young man already. He had personality, and reminded her of her younger brother.

Karen walked over to the table, shook Bruce's hand, and sat down. They shared a few minutes of small talk. She found out that Bruce had planned a camping trip with his fiancé for the weekend. Karen had plans to meet her family for an outing herself, but, like always, work came first. Once again, Karen mentally questioned Terry's choice of timing for the interview. Scheduling an interview on the Friday of a holiday weekend was an interesting choice.

When it was apparent that Terry was not going to show, Karen started in with the official interview. Bruce was impressive. Karen was pleased that the interview had gone so well, and thought Bruce would be an excellent addition to the company. She was wrapping up the interview so that Bruce could get back home and pack for his camping trip when suddenly Terry stumbled into the restaurant. Karen was shocked to see how intoxicated Terry was. Not only was she shocked, she was also quite embarrassed. Being a seasoned HR professional, she knew that not only was the job candidate being judged for the position; the company was also being scrutinized by the candidate. She thought that Terry had probably blown Bruce's desire to come to work for them.

Terry sat down in the chair next to Bruce, sending a wave of Scotch aroma their way. Every time Terry would say something to Bruce he would turn his head in the opposite direction, trying to prevent Bruce from smelling his breath. After about two minutes of talking, Terry said, "You are hired! Let's go." Bruce asked, "Go where?" Terry replied "Eastport". Eastport was the local bar district. Karen thought there was no way she could allow Bruce to get into the car with Terry. She had to think fast. How could she stop this without embarrassing her boss? She decided she simply had to jump in. She informed Terry that Bruce had plans, and that maybe they could celebrate later. Karen was also thinking that there was no way she could let her boss drive anywhere in such an inebriated state.

Karen asked Terry to wait at the table while she escorted Bruce to the door. On the way to the door Karen apologized to Bruce for the situation, and told him that they would be back in touch with him after the holiday. She was hoping he would still accept the job. Bruce's response was, "That is okay, but I do think this is worth about a $3,000 increase to the offer you are going to propose." He smiled and left.

Yes, Bruce did accept the job at $3,000 more than the original offer.

~~~~~~~~~~~~~~~~~~~~~~~~~~~~~~~~~~~~~~~~~~~~~~~~~

"People have the power to redeem the work of fools."
~ Patti Smith

"Sometimes it is better to be a no show than a dumb show."
~ Joy Dye

# DON'T BE IN SUCH A HURRY

## "I won't mention your pants, you don't mention my hair."

Mary did not wear a dress to work very often. Most of the time she wore a pantsuit, simply because it was more comfortable than putting on a pair of panty hose and wearing heels. However, there was a new guy at the office, and Mary was a little interested in him. His name was Mike. He was the cutest guy she had ever seen, with dark, wavy hair, and green eyes. She had noticed his good looks first, but when she saw him go out of his way to open the door for the janitor one day, and the deal was sealed. Her heart was drawn to him. He had just graduated from MU, and looked to be a successful executive in the making. In her daydreams she pictured herself living in a two-story, brick house with two kids and a dog—with Mike. Okay, so she had more than just a little interest in him—she had a full-blown schoolgirl crush. Mary was determined to get his attention.

On Wednesday Mary was scheduled to present the roll-out plan for a new software program they were installing. Most of the managers would be present at the meeting, including Mike. Mary thought this was an opportunity to get Mike's attention. The meeting was scheduled to last an hour. This would be an hour that could be the beginning of their story. The story they would tell their kids on how they met. The story of the day Mike first asked her out. Yes, this could be the most important hour of her life.

Tuesday after work, Mary went shopping for the perfect dress to wear the next day to work. It had been a long time since she actually pursued a man; in fact she had never really put much effort into that game. Most of the time men would try to gain her attention. But this time, the hunt was on for a dress that would gain the attention of her heartthrob, Mike. She wanted a blue dress, one that would match her eyes and flatter her small waist. After two hours of spinning through store after store at the mall she found it. A blue silk wrap that hung perfectly around her slender form escorted her to the checkout.

On Wednesday she wore the blue dress, hose, heels, and even curled her hair. As she dashed out the door she even sprayed a little perfume on her wrist. She had to admit she felt like a knockout walking into the office that day. She got a lot of compliments, and thought that maybe she should start dressing this way more often. Her friends jokingly asked if she had a job interview or something.

The software presentation was scheduled for 4:00 PM. Mary had just enough time to take a quick trip to the bathroom before running into the conference room where she would be showing her PowerPoint. Her belly was a little queasy from thinking about Mike being in the audience. She had not felt like this since high school. She walked into the conference room and took her place in the front. After everyone had taken their seats, she thanked them for coming, and then commenced to give a wonderful presentation. She did a fine job. She did not stumble on her words, or forget her place, or have technical problems with the computer. She finished up right at 5:00. Perfect timing! She was very proud that she had nailed it. There was nothing that she would have done differently. Everyone left the conference room to head home as Mary stayed behind to clean up. After everyone had left, Mary decided to sit down for just a bit before taking down the computer. As she slid her hand along her backside to sit, she did not feel her dress, she felt her panty hose. What was this? Oh, my gosh! In her earlier haste in the bathroom, she had accidently gotten her dress tucked inside her panty hose. She had given her presentation with the back of her dress tucked in her panty hose.

Well, she could probably still have the two-story brick house with two kids someday—it just probably would not be with Mike.

~~~~~~~~~~~~~~~~~~~~~~~~~~~~~~~~~~~~~~~~~~~~~~

"To an adolescent, there is nothing in the world more
embarrassing than a parent."
~ Dave Barry

"But I learned that there's a certain character that can be
built from embarrassing yourself endlessly. If you can sit
happy with embarrassment, there's not much else that can
really get to ya."
~ Christian Bale

29

# PICK A PARTNER LIKE A SPOUSE

## "We're here on a mission of mercy ... to mercilessly kill this company."

Lisa and Carol sat on the bleachers, watching their daughters play softball together. Lisa's daughter was the pitcher, and Carol's played first base. Their team was called *The Xtreme*, and was very competitive. With two metro championships on their record, it looked like this year could end in a state championship. Nationals would be played in Orlando. The younger siblings of the players were really looking forward to that possibility. The parents of *The Xtreme* scheduled their family vacations around the various tournaments to which the team had been invited to play. Last weekend they played in Dallas, and next week there would be a four-day trip to Amarillo. The team, the parents, the coaches, and the siblings were like a small traveling city. The group became best friends, an extended family really.

Carol had a small data management company, ODS. She had started ODS as a way to be able to stay home with her children and still contribute to the family's income. Lisa was working on a software program to help her husband's pool cleaning company deal with OSHA and DOL compliance. Lisa thought she had a great product, but needed a little help with marketing, and servicing future customers. Carol had the contacts and the business experience that Lisa needed. At one of the softball games Lisa approached Carol and asked if she would like to start a partnership.

After many visits to the local coffee shop, and several hand scribbled notes later, *Cameo Consultants* was born. Lisa owned the majority of the company, because she put the most capital into it. Both ladies built the company with true blood, sweat, and tears. After nine years their company had grown to having five employees and 20 clients, but had hit a plateau. It seemed to have stalled out. Lisa was starting to show signs of wanting out, but Carol was still full of energy, and thought they had a good thing going.

One day, while leaving the office for lunch, Lisa announced to Carol, "I am majority stock holder in the company and I have found a buyer for *Cameo*. I think I am going to sell the company." Then she abruptly left. Carol was numb. What had Lisa said? She was thinking about selling the company, without even talking to her? Carol chased after Lisa into the parking lot, but was unable to catch her. Of course, Lisa did not come back to the office that afternoon.

The next day at the office, Lisa had explained to Carol that she wanted out. She just did not know how to exit gracefully, so she did the only thing she knew—she found a buyer. She told Carol not to worry. She was trying to work out a deal that would pay them well, and that would leave them both with a job with the new company. Carol asked, "What about our employees?" Lisa said, "They will be okay. This kind of thing happens every day." Lisa then handed Carol a $50.00 gift card to a local salon. She said, "Here, go get a massage. It will release some of the stress." Carol was not much for self-indulgences, and put the gift card in her wallet.

31

Lisa had the deal with the new owner more advanced than Carol thought. Carol learned that the plan Lisa had agreed to included a position for them both with the new company. Carol would not be an owner, just an employee. Carol would be forced to sign a non-compete clause. Lisa, on the other hand, would be part-owner of the new company. Lisa's office was lush, with three windows, mahogany office furniture, and enough space for a conference table and sitting area. Carol's office was a very small, a second thought spot, with the community copier/printer practically rubbing up against the back of her chair. Her new salary would be $10,000 less than what it was with the old *Cameo*. Carol also found her next paycheck to be $50.00 short—the exact amount of the "gift" card that Lisa had given her. Carol also found out that the capital Lisa used to start *Cameo* several years ago was money she had borrowed from her parents. Nice—borrowing money from your parents does not always require official paperwork. Lisa told Carol that she had borrowed $50,000 from her parents at 30% interest, and it would was expected that her parents would be reimbursed, with interest, out of the profits of the sale of the company. Carol began to see the evil that lived inside Lisa. 30%!? Was she crazy? A bank loan would not be that high. This evil plot was just one way for Lisa to capture more of the profits of the sale of the company they both built.

Carol did not like the details on sale of the company, but she had no choice but to go along with Lisa's plan. Carol had talked with an attorney, and was advised that she could sue for "oppression of minority stock holder". Carol did not even want to think about suing Lisa. They were close friends, for goodness sake! Carol had to trust that Lisa would treat her fairly in the sale of their company.

Carol was in shock. The sale of the company went through. *George's Safety Consultants* now owned *Cameo Consultants*. After taking the money Lisa promised to give back to her parents, and giving their employees' severance pay, Carol's grand cut of selling nine years of her labor came to a whopping $55,000. Not much for nine years of blood, sweat, and tears. Carol went ahead and played the game just to see where it would take her. What choice did she have? She showed up at her new office on Monday. She kept a positive attitude through the first week.

In the second week Lisa had asked Carol to set up the conference room to run a demo of their software package for all the employees of *George's Safety Consultants*. Carol started setting up the demo at 11:30. At 12:00 things were ready and Carol sat patiently and waited. Finally at 1:00 Carol went to seek Lisa out. Nobody had shown up for the demo and Carol was thinking that maybe Lisa had the wrong date. When Carol finally found Lisa, she was in the lunchroom finishing eating pizza with all the new employees. It was obvious. There was no demo scheduled. Lisa had just wanted Carol out of the way while she had pizza with the new employees.

The next day Lisa told Carol that she needed her to meet with a new client at a coffee shop and run a demo on the software for him. Obediently, Carol went to the coffee shop to meet with the new client. The new client never showed. When Carol got back to the office she found that the new owner, George, had just finished a meeting with the entire staff, welcoming *Cameo Consultants* onboard. Once again, Lisa had lied just to make sure Carol was not part of the relationship building with the new company. Carol had had enough. She quit. She thought about giving notice, but at this point she was just too angry.

Carol thought about contacting her attorney again, but she just honestly wanted to put this behind her. She had been raised to not take revenge. That was God's job, and He would do a much better job at that than Carol ever could.

A few days later Carol went to the salon to use the gift card Lisa had "given" to her and Carol had ultimately paid for. Instead of a massage, Carol got her hair cut. A new hairdo would be just what she needed to start on a new career path. When Carol went to pay for the haircut she pulled out the gift card. When the cashier ran it through the register she said, "I'm sorry but this gift card has already been used."

Carol would never again start a business with a partner and give so much of herself. Lisa's new relationship with George lasted only about three months. George quickly learned the type of person that Lisa was, and acted on a clause in the contract allowing him to stop the purchase of *Cameo*. George then called Carol and asked if she would like to come to work for him. Yes, what goes around comes around.

~~~~~~~~~~~~~~~~~~~~~~~~~~~~~~~~~~~~~~~~~~~~~~~

Do not take revenge, my friends, but leave room for God's wrath, for it is written: "It is mine to avenge; I will repay," says the Lord.
~ Romans 12:19

"Never lose sight of the fact that the most important yardstick of your success will be how you treat other people—your family, friends, and coworkers, and even strangers you meet along the way."
~ Barbara Bush

# "Has the window washer seemed disgruntled?"

Teresa was the Office Manager for a shoe company in Dallas. She ran their local office of 20 employees very smoothly. She was the main contact for their corporate office in Washington. She had held the position for 10 years, and was ready to advance in the company. The Division Vice President was her boss, Rob. He would be retiring in one month. She had applied for his position, but upper management had decided to offer the position to an outside person. Teresa had all the qualifications for the position, but they said they were bringing in someone with "fresh eyes." Teresa was extremely disappointed, but she was a team player, and would do what she could to help with the transition. Her company's top management was relying on her to help Rob's replacement learn the finer details of his job. The new Division Vice President would have one month with Rob, and then would be expected to hit the ground running.

On Monday morning Rob's replacement, David, arrived. He was very pleasant, and Teresa thought this was going to work out just fine. She would miss Rob, but David seemed to be a good fit. Teresa would see the two men walking back into the office after lunch talking and laughing. They seemed like old friends. One day David even stopped to comment on a shoe-shaped clock in the lobby. Rob said he could not resist buying it as a gift for the office, thinking it was a perfect fit for their company. David also said he liked the pale green walls in Rob's office, that they were calming. The month David spent with Rob went by quickly. Rob was comfortable that David could handle the position and felt good about retiring.

The day of Rob's retirement party was bittersweet. There were a lot of hugs and tears and memories shared. Everyone loved Rob, and he would be missed. Teresa helped Rob carry his final box of personal belongings to his car. She gave him a hug and told him he was the best boss she had ever had. As she waved goodbye to Rob she had butterflies in her stomach. She looked to the future with excitement, anticipation, and anxiety. She had been comfortable with Rob as her boss. David would be okay; just different, that's all. She did not really care for changes.

Monday morning was David's first day in the office as Division Vice President. He took command! It was like someone had flipped a switch on David. What had once been a team atmosphere in the office suddenly turned into a dictatorship. On David's first day he implemented a policy that employees could not eat at their desks anymore. Then he cut out all smoking breaks, and put in a time clock. Before the change everyone had simply submitted their time on a spreadsheet to their manager for approval. David said he did not trust the staff to be honest with their time, and punching time cards would ensure honesty. David then had Teresa submit a work order to their Maintenance Department to paint his office tan. He could not stand working in a pale green office, saying it made him nauseous.

David was demanding of Teresa's time. Teresa was salaried, but David abused her time 24 hours a day, 7 days a week. He expected her to be at the office before he arrived in the morning, and not leave until after he was gone in the evening. He would call her into the office on weekends for issues that could wait until Monday. He expected her to bring him coffee every morning, and order his lunch if he did not plan on going out. Teresa had just about had it with the change in command. She knew the job market was hard, but she started to look to see what else was out there. The office she had grown to love so much had turned into a place that she loathed. She would wait until she found something else, and then give her two-week notice.

One morning after Teresa had gotten her cup of coffee and was settling into her desk, she looked up and saw David taking down the shoe clock. She caught David's eye and looked at him questioningly. David said, "I never did like that stupid clock. It gave the office an unprofessional atmosphere." Teresa had had enough! She said, "That is it! That is the final straw! I quit!" Everyone looked up from their desks in surprise. Teresa grabbed her jacket and stormed out of the office.

Half way to her car she realized she left her purse at her desk with her car keys. Sheepishly she walked back into the office, red faced. She walked to her desk, grabbed her purse and said, "Okay, NOW I quit."

~~~~~~~~~~~~~~~~~~~~~~~~~~~~~~~~~~~~~~~~~~~

"A quick temper will make a fool of you soon enough."
~ Bruce Lee

"It is not necessary to change because your survival is not mandatory."
~ W. Edwards Deming

# A STICKY SITUATION

## "Everything was fine until you insisted on accountability."

This story comes from our archives. In the days before computers, cell phones, and iPods, there was a young secretary named Barbara. She worked hard at her job. Dictation and typing were her strong skills. She was still getting used to the electric typewriter that her boss had recently purchased for the office. It was a Selectric model 350. Barbara thought it was the best invention ever. It actually had a memory, and she could make it erase the last 35 letters that she had typed. Finally she could throw away her liquid correction fluid.

Barb was expecting a particularly busy month, with the year-end reports that she would have to write, in addition to all her normal day-to-day responsibilities. Barb was the only secretary for an office of 15. Her husband always told her that they kept her busier than a one-armed wallpaper hanger. Barb's boss did not want to pay Barb overtime for the additional work, but he did agree to bring in a temporary to help for one month. Barb was relieved when her boss had finally agreed to temporary help. Barb called the temp agency and requested someone with office experience. The job would not be difficult, simply typing and filing.

The next day Barb arrived at the office early. She wanted to make sure everything was caught up, so that she would be able to spend the day training the temporary. She expected the second day on the job for the temp to be productive. At 9:00 AM the temporary employee, Darcie, arrived at the office. Right away Barb had a feeling that Darcie was not accustomed to doing much office work. Darcie had very long fingernails; much too long to be serious typist. Darcie obviously spent a lot of time at the beauty salon. Every hair was teased and sprayed, and her makeup was flawless. Darcie's heels clicked across the hard wood floor as she walked up to Barb's desk. A wave if Chanel #5 invaded Barb's sinus cavity. Darcie had a walk that would turn any man's head. Barb welcomed her with a warm smile and offered to get her a cup of coffee. Darcie asked if they had caramel syrup to drizzle in her coffee. With eyebrows raised Barb said, "Sorry Darcie, all we have is cream and sugar." Then Barb thought, "Caramel syrup? Who would put something like that in coffee?"

Barb got to work right away teaching Darcie where things were stored, what to do with the mail, and where the file cabinets were located. The first task Barb gave Darcie was to type labels for the mailboxes. She gave Darcie a list with the names of the 15 office employees and a sheet of labels. Barb then left to go to the filing room to pull the folders she would need to do her year-end reports.

After 15 minutes, Barb went to check on Darcie. When she walked up to Darcie's desk, she had to hold back a gasp, then a laugh. Darcie was peeling the labels off the sheet, placing them on the typewriter roller, typing the name, and then peeling the label off the roller and placing the sticker back on the sheet of labels.

Maybe Barb would have been more productive without temporary help. Maybe Barb's boss would start reconsidering paying overtime. Maybe Darcie should have opened the countries first coffee shop offering indulgent ingredients to each cup.

~~~~~~~~~~~~~~~~~~~~~~~~~~~~~~~~~~~~~~~~~~~~~~~

"Always be nice to secretaries. They are the real
gatekeepers in the world."
~ Anthony J. D'Angelo

"Our differences in judgment or actions are rarely due to
stupidity, but more from background and education, so be
nice to those that amuse you."
~Joy Dye

# IT HAPPENS TO THE BEST OF US

## "Am I the only one who remembered '50's Friday?"

Tony had just completed his time as an intern at *South Parker Hospital*, and was ready to start his first day in family practice with a new medical group in town—the *Pine Park Family Medical Center*. Tony had worked very hard. Most people do not realize how hard a residency is, with the stress, the lack of sleep, and the anxious thoughts of what could happen if a mistake was made. It was not an easy road by any definition. But he had made it! He was ready to face the world with the profession he had chosen and worked very hard toward obtaining.

He was ready for a career in the profession of saving lives. He was a General Practitioner, specializing in family medicine.

Tony always felt a little uncomfortable when he first met a stranger. As soon as they found out he was a "doctor" they would say, "Oh, a doctor huh?" and then look at him like they expected him to have all the answers that would save the world. Tony was human, for goodness sake! He laughed at jokes, especially when they came unexpectedly. He cried at sad movies (when he was alone, of course). He liked a night out with the guys, and a good game of poker. He loved to spend time with his girlfriend, and appreciated the peace she brought to his hectic life.

On Monday morning the alarm went off at 6:00 AM. Tony got up and showered, then dressed in his pressed pants and shirt. To make his look complete, he put on a tie his girlfriend had given him to start his new job. He gulped down a quick glass of milk, and grabbed a donut as he headed out the door to *Pine Park Family Medical Center*. He hopped into his 10-year-old Pathfinder and thought, "Just a few more months and a new car could possibly be in my driveway." Nobody in his family had ever owned a new car before. He was excited at the thought of that new car smell, shiny wheels, and leather seats. Tony did not spend money on too many things, but after spending several years in medical school, and then his residency, a new car seemed well deserved.

He was a little nervous when he arrived at the clinic. The ladies at the front desk were expecting him and put him at ease right away. He walked into his office, which he and his girlfriend had just finished decorating that weekend. He noticed on his desk a plant and card left by the staff. It was their welcome to the practice present. It made him feel comfortable and at home, ready to make a long career with them. Smiling at a framed photograph on his desk, he put his two fingers to his lips, pressed them against the glass on the picture of his girlfriend, grabbed his white lab coat, and went off to visit his first patient.

His first patient was a five-year-old boy with a headache and the sniffles. When he walked into the exam room he introduced himself first to the little boy, and then to the boy's mother. He checked the boy's chart, and the vitals the nurse had taken earlier. He looked at his throat, in his ears, and listened to the faint rattle in his pint-sized chest. After his evaluation, Tony had determined that the little boy had an infection that was starting to irritate his lungs. A prescription for Amoxicillin would help him fight it off. Tony explained to the mother what he had determined, checked for any allergies, and ordered the medicine over the computer. The mother could pick up the medicine for her little boy at her chosen pharmacy within a few hours. If things did not improve in one week she was instructed to bring her son back.

Tony shook hands with the mom and little boy, told them goodbye, and advised that the little boy wash his hands before eating. This was something that Tony had gotten into the habit of telling all his patients. Tony opened the door, backed out of the room and shut the door. Suddenly Tony realized he walked into the exam-room closet!

He could have opened the door, stepped back into the room and left through the door that lead to the hallway, but he would not be able to live down the embarrassment. Instead, Tony stayed in the closet until he heard the mom and little boy leave. Then he quietly left the patient's room, hoping the little boy and mom did not notice, and if they did, hoping they would not say anything.

Yes, doctors are human too.

~~~~~~~~~~~~~~~~~~~~~~~~~~~~~~~~~~~~~~~~~~~~~~~

"People pay the doctor for his trouble; for his kindness they
still remain in his debt."
~ Seneca

"The more you can laugh at your own mistakes, the smaller
they become."
~Joy Dye

# SAY WHAT?

## "Your job is to fire everyone except you ... for now."

*OLC* was a company that provided phone sales for top name-brand companies. It had grown rapidly, going from 52 employees to 2,000 in ten years. During the company's infancy the management team had focused its energy on building relationships and advertising. The strong ties that grew from these efforts had propelled *OLC* out in front of their competition, and they had developed a strong reputation. Phone sales generally carry an unspoken push back from companies, but not with *OLC*. Their sales force put their personal relationships first and the business relationships second. A few tickets to a football game, concert, or dinner theater would generally lead to an annual contract. In this world of web meetings, voice-mails, and e-mails, it was that face-to-face contact that seemed to be the secret of their success.

Linda was excited about her new job in the Human Resources Department for *OLC*. Her college years had gone by very fast.

Fresh out of college, with a Bachelor's degree in Business, she could still hear the echo of the graduation orchestra playing "Pomp and Circumstance". Her stomach felt a tinge of excitement while walking through the glass doors into the marble-floored lobby of OLC. Linda was not sure what Human Resources was all about, but she was eager to learn. While serving as President of her college sorority there had been little she could not handle, and she was sure she could take on all the challenges of this new job head-on. Of course, she would plan on calling home once in a while, just to grease her confidence and tighten her career decision with kind, encouraging words from her parents.

Linda's first week on the job was taxing on her memory. She had to learn so much, and finally came to understand the difference between FMLA and Workman's Compensation. She had frequently heard those terms, but now could actually have an intelligent conversation with staff about them. Learning the difference between an HSA and other insurance programs, as well as the difference between a deductible and a co-pay was not easy. Previously, being covered by her parents' plan, such matters had not concerned her. All that she needed to know before was where to find her insurance card before heading to a doctor's appointment. Now things were changing for Linda. She was becoming independent. She had her own apartment, paid her own deposit on utilities, and was saving up to buy a car. She was becoming a responsible adult. Yes, she was stepping into adulthood with bright eyes, a straight posture, and a clear mind.

Linda quickly made a new friend in her co-worker Marcie. Marcie had a candor about her that was warm, yet to the point. She was professional when she had to be, but preferred a silly adolescent approach to problems. She used words like *knucklehead* and *humdinger*. Linda would laugh to herself every time those words came out of Marcie's mouth. Marcie had been the one assigned to train Linda. Actually, Marcie had volunteered. She loved to help out the newbies. There was a lot for Linda to learn. One of the monthly tasks was to assemble the termination packages. When OLC lost an employee, either through a resignation or a termination, the Human Resources Department would handle all the voluminous, tedious paperwork. Marcie quickly walked Linda through the process of putting the termination packages together before Marcie had to run off to a meeting. Linda was told to include the COBRA information, along with the exit interview letter, and a letter summarizing the dismissed employee's service record. Marcie gave Linda a list of the nine employees that had recently been dismissed, and who needed the packets mailed to their homes. The instructions from Marcie were very quick but thorough. Marcie handed Linda a list of names for her check off sheet, and then with a, "Catch ya later, alligator," left for her meeting. Linda was left on her own to finish the job.

Linda was proud of the job she had done. Everything was in order. She had double checked the contents of the packets, and printed off the mailing labels. She took the nine large brown envelopes down the three flights of stairs to the mailroom to be sent out. On the way back, Linda stopped by the break room to grab a candy bar, a small reward for a job well done. She then scampered back upstairs to do her filing.

David Weber had worked at OLC for six years. His last performance review had been disappointing, but he thought that he had improved his performance over the last four months. His boss told him to work on his time management and communication skills. David made an effort to become more organized. He started making a to-do list, and checked off items as they were completed. He also found himself taking extra steps to make sure he was clear and to the point in his e-mails and voice-mails. He also had his 15-year-old nephew show him how to set calendar alerts on his phone. His last performance review slapped hard. He knew that if changes were not made in his performance he would probably be given his walking papers. He was trying his best to polish his act.

David lived down a gravel road, so he had to pick up his mail at the post office in town. On Saturday morning David and his wife made their routine 15-mile trip into town. He dropped his wife off at the grocery store and drove to the post office. In his box he found a large brown envelope from OLC. Curious, he opened it right there in the lobby. He felt a little funny at first, opening his mail in public. Normally he waited to take care of things like this at home. He thought the lady that ran the post office was a little nosey. She would talk with him about things that were none of her business, things like the Johnsons coming for a weekend visit, or about how his brother was thinking of running for public office. These were things that were only mentioned in letters between David and his brother. David swore she probably opened his mail just to get the scoop. At times he actually found himself inspecting his letters for illegal entry.

But for now the letter from OLC pushed all reservation aside. What was this? Instructions for an exit interview, COBRA information, and a service letter? Had he been fired? Was this how OLC fired people? Thoughts rushed through David's head. What had he done wrong lately? He and his boss just talked about how he was improving. Was this the major layoff that was rumored? What would he tell his wife? The job market was tough right now. Why hadn't he finished college when he had a chance? David had just turned 46, and he knew that people his age were at a disadvantage when competing for jobs. David looked for a trash can to throw up in. His stomach was turning flips, and he was breaking out in a cold sweat.

Panicked, David raced to his car to get his cell phone. He called Mike, his best friend and co-worker. Mike could not believe David got fired—and like this! Mike told David he would be over that night to help him think this through. David's drive home with his wife was long, suffocating and silent. Except for a few sobs from his wife, the only sound was an occasional backfire from the old dented pickup, a V-6 that drank oil like a sponge, and smelled like minnow water. The fact that his wife was crying made the taste in David's mouth even more bitter. Worry plopped down on both of them like a two-ton elephant. David found it hard to breathe.

That night, Mike showed up at David's with a six-pack and a bag of chips. Mike and David spent the night on David's deck talking about life, the next steps to take, and the possibilities that Mike could be next on the chopping block. David was glad to have Mike as a friend. If nothing else, he was truly blessed to have a real friend who would help carry a burden like this.

The weekend was the longest of David's life. Sunday morning at church, during the men's study class, David asked for everyone to keep him in their prayers while he looked for a new job. Their lesson was appropriately on the story of Job, a man who lost everything, but was eventually blessed beyond measure. David hoped his story had the same blessed ending.

David wrote a letter to his bank asking if they could rework the loan on his house until he was employed again. David thought a letter would be better than a face-to-face visit with his loan officer. If he put his request in writing, they would have to write back, and somehow that would be less embarrassing than having them say, "No!" to his face. His rival from high school football, Mark Powonoski, was the bank President. Even though it had been decades since they graduated from high school, the competitive edge between them was still detectable. It was going to be an uncomfortable moment the next time David ran into Mark in town.

Then finally David had to call his parents. David had planned on taking his parents and wife on a cruise that summer. This was probably the last summer that would work for everyone, because his parents' health was starting to decline. Telling his parents that he had been fired was hard. David felt he had let them down. They had always been very proud of their son. Next he called the travel agent, cancelling their cruise and losing his deposit.

Monday morning came and David slept in. No need to get up today. With no job to go to, sleeping in was the only positive he could take from all of this. At 8:30 AM David's phone rang. In his stupor, David reached for the phone, knocking the alarm clock to the floor. "Hello?" said David, trying to clear his dry throat. "David, where are you?" came a concerned voice on the other end. David recognized the voice of Mr. Ryan, his boss. Confused, David said, "I was fired." Mr. Ryan said "What? No, you weren't. I don't know what kind of joke this is but get to the office as soon as you can. We have an important meeting at 9:00, and you are presenting, remember?" David did not question his boss. He frantically dressed and arrived at the office 25 minutes later. David gave the presentation, one of the best of his life; but there was still a sense of confusion in his mind. After everyone had cleared the conference room, David marched right into the Human Resources office.

David handed the lady behind the desk, Linda, the brown envelope he had received in the mail on Saturday. He asked for an explanation. After researching the situation Linda discovered that David Webber was the employee on the dismissal list—not David Weber.

~~~~~~~~~~~~~~~~~~~~~~~~~~~~~~~~~~~~~~~~~~~~~~~

"We made too many wrong mistakes."
~ Yogi Berra

"The best way to appreciate your job is to imagine yourself without one."
~Oscar Wilde

49

# I DON'T DO WINDOWS

# "Having live-in tech support is very reassuring."

Everyone took their turn at doing the odd chores at *Gerald's Appliance Repair*. The lunchroom was a community area. If you used the microwave, you were expected to clean it. If the coffee pot was empty, you were expected to refill it. The employees also took turns washing the coffee cups at the end of the day. A list was posted on the refrigerator so dish duty was fair and you knew when it was your turn. It worked well because everyone took part and helped out.

Julie was new to the team. She had grown up privileged, and had never broken a sweat at hard labor. She was nice, and did an adequate job as Accounts Payable Clerk, but she was not sure about sharing the chores of the lunchroom. She had grown up on a successful estate and horse ranch, where they had raised and trained several champion racehorses. She had a maid, a cook, and a driver. She would fly to London to shop (first class, of course), and never missed the social events of her highbrow community. Her father had insisted that she get a job, for a couple of years at least. He said that learning what it was like to earn a living would make her become a better person. Julie thought she already *was* a good person, but could not stand toe-to-toe with her dad and argue.

She got along just fine with the girls in the office. They were a little different from her, but very welcoming. Pam sat in the cubicle next to Julie's, but seemed to be of a different breed. Pam was an Air Force brat. While Pam did get to see a lot of the world while growing up, it was never just for fun and relaxation. During Pam's father's service he had been stationed in England, Scotland, Thailand, and Hawaii. He moved his family with him every time. Pam grew up putting her pennies in her piggy bank, saving for a rainy day. She knew hard work, how to cook, and how to fold a fitted bed sheet.

Pam and Julie had planned to go get manicures, or *mannies* (as Julie called them), after work. It had been a long, hard day, and Pam was looking forward to spending some time with Julie. They had not really had a chance to "talk" since Julie had joined the company two months ago. Five o'clock finally came. Pam told Julie that she had to drop some things off in the mailroom, and would meet her in the lunchroom. She offered to drive to the nail salon.

Pam dropped her items off in the mailroom, and made her way back to the lunchroom. There she found Julie loading the dirty coffee cups from the day into a cardboard box. Pam asked, "Julie, what cha doin?" Julie said, "I am taking the coffee cups home to load them in the dishwasher. It is my turn to wash dishes."

*Karla O'Malley*

You can take the girl off the estate, but you can't take the estate out of the girl!

~~~~~~~~~~~~~~~~~~~~~~~~~~~~~~~~~~~~~~~~~~~~

"All life demands struggle. Those who have everything
given to them become lazy, selfish, and insensitive to the
real values of life. The very striving and hard work that we
so constantly try to avoid is the major building block in the
person we are today."
~ Pope John Paul II

"Hard work spotlights the character of people: some turn up
their sleeves, some turn up their noses, and some don't turn
up at all."
~Sam Ewing

# NO SHOW

## "Yes, we are a thriving law firm ... look, a bent but still usable staple!"

Dan was an interesting entrepreneur, to say the least. He came from a long line of successful business people. To shimmy up his family tree would be to visit inventors, politicians, and business owners. The old saying *a penny saved is a penny earned* did not make much sense in Dan's family. Why would anyone worry about saving a penny when you routinely used Grants and Franklins as waitress' tip money? With the wealth of his family heritage, Dan was free to "play" the game of life. Money was not something to worry about. It seemed he had an eternal supply of the green.

Dan owned a small company in Iowa. His company was located in a seedy part of town, the part of town where land was cheap and misery was plentiful. Nobody wanted to work or live in that area. The air had the smell of moldy, wet paper from a nearby recycling plant, and depression hung in the air like a low cloud. This cloud was so heavy that it seemed to have the residents in a Full-Nelson, unwilling to allow them to wiggle out of the city limits. Just north of Dan's main office building was a muddy river, and just south was a set of active railroad tracks. These tracks screamed the evidence that there was life and prosperity outside of this town. In the otherwise ignored thick clump of woods between the river and the tracks was a homeless camp, a camp where a black hole of despair quickly snatched hopes and dreams out of the thoughts of its inhabitants. The camp was located about two miles west of Dan's office.

Dan lived with the idea that he could change the lives of people in need, and he occasionally did. It was not unusual for Dan to see some of the homeless population standing on street corners holding signs of desperation. Dan would sometimes hand the person on the corner a dollar or two out of the change bin of his Lincoln Navigator.

Carol was Dan's Director of Human Resources. She understood Dan's inner desire to help others, but sometimes his actions went around company protocol and human logic. Dan's actions generally ignored all Human Resource standards, but it was his company, and his money. Carol could not do or say anything but support Dan. His optimism was admirable, yet naïve.

One day, when Dan was on his way home, he spied yet another homeless person standing on the street corner holding a sign. The young man's name was Henry. Dan stopped and asked if he was hungry. Henry smiled a toothless, dirty smile and said, "Yeth thir!" Dan told Henry to hop in, and drove Henry to the local hamburger joint. Dan and Henry sat across the table from each other at the restaurant enjoying their meals and getting to know each other. Henry said that he had a wife and child back at the homeless camp. Henry told Dan that he had just been laid off from a job at the local auto plant, and that he was very eager to work again. Dan asked if Henry would like to go to work at his company, and Henry said "Yeth thir!"

Dan was taken in by Henry's story. Dan called Carol and told her that Henry would be at the office in the morning. Dan did not care what job Carol found for him, but he wanted her to find something that they could hire him to do full time. Dan paused in his phone conversation with Carol. He placed his hand over the receiver of the phone, turned to Henry and said, "You can pass a drug test, can't you Henry?" Henry said, "Yeth thir!" There, that was settled. Dan was giving Henry a job. It would change life for Henry, and he would be able to provide a decent life for his wife and child.

Dan and Henry finished their hamburgers and fries, then headed back to Dan's Lincoln. Dan drove Henry back to his corner. Before Henry got out of the car, Dan handed Henry $100.00 in cash and told him he would see him in the morning. Henry smiled, took the money and said, "Yeth thir!" Dan drove home with a fulfilled smile on his face. He felt that this day was one worth getting out of bed for. He had just helped change someone's life.

The next day, guess who did not show up for work—Henry. The night before, guess who had paid for the entire homeless camp to have a party—Dan. Guess who just shook her head and said, "Just another day at the office."—Carol.

~~~~~~~~~~~~~~~~~~~~~~~~~~~~~~~~~~~~~~~~~~~~~~~

"All motivation is self-motivation. Your family, your boss, or
your co-workers can try to get your engine going, but until
you decide what to accomplish, nothing will happen."
~ Seth Godin

"Human Resources is the silent mom, police, psychiatrist,
nurse and teacher of the office."
~ Joy Dye

# THE HAIR OF THE DOG

## "Go easy on me. I just had my annual review."

Max was a Golden Retriever that had been a very good addition to the family that Christmas morning 10 years ago. He happily joined the ranks of the O'Reilly family. Carl O'Reilly held the responsibility of CEO and Dad of the household. Teresa was Chief Cook and Mom, while Mary held the position of Senior Kiddo, followed by Rick and Jeff as her support staff, or kid brothers. Max fit right in, and took his place proudly in family photos, while protecting their property from the mailman on a daily basis.

Max was a very smart dog. He had several tricks in his bag. He could do the elementary tricks of sit, roll over, and shake. He was also an Ivy League dog who knew how to balance a bone on his nose, and bark in a whisper. Yes, Max was a great dog.

But like most dogs, Max would shed. His owners had to vacuum daily just to keep up with the clumps of golden hair that could be found throughout the house. Max also occasionally needed a bath. Whenever Max heard the water running in the bathtub, he would hide. One time he almost got away with hiding in one of the closets. Jeff, the dutiful bath giver, started the routine hide-and-seek game of finding Max after the bath water was ready for him. Jeff looked in Max's usual hiding places. He checked behind the couch, under the office desk and peered into the coat closet. Just as Jeff had given up, he heard a little growl coming out of the closet. Yes, Max had given himself up to the enemy, and was "bravely dragged" to the bathtub.

Teresa had been in the job market for some time. She had worked as an administrative assistant at a car plant that closed eight months earlier. She spent every day checking websites and papers for job openings. There seemed to be a good number of job openings that fit her skills, but the number of applicants was daunting. Job hunting made her feel like she was draining a pond with a ladle. She had a few phone interviews, but they never resulted in face-to-face interviews.

One evening, on his way home from the office, Carl stopped and bought Teresa a beautiful black pantsuit. Carl had noticed her eyeing it through the window of a local store while on one of their evening walks. He knew that Teresa was starting to get frustrated in her job search, and he thought this would cheer her up.

Carl walked through the front door that evening, pantsuit in hand. Teresa was anxiously waiting for him to arrive, almost jumping out of her shoes with excitement! *Grainer's Insurance Company* had called her that day for a face-to-face interview the next day. With that said, Carl handed her the beautiful pantsuit, saying, "Great, you will look wonderful in this for your interview." He handed her the pantsuit that was hung ever so carefully on a padded hanger and draped with a protective plastic bag. "How did you know?" Teresa asked. Carl just grinned and pretended he had a feeling about today.

The next day Teresa found that time had slipped away from her. She had done all the normal chores, then glanced at the clock. She had only one hour to get ready for her interview and get out the door. Quickly she showered, washed and dried her hair, and put on her makeup. She then put on her new pantsuit, with a crisp white shirt, and pearl necklace. She looked awesome. If they hired based on appearance, she would definitely get the job. As she reached for her light coat from the hall tree, she noticed that it had fallen to the floor. She grabbed it, put it on, and was out the door in a flash.

Teresa arrived at *Grainer's Insurance* confident, yet nervously excited. She said a small prayer before getting out of the car. Teresa walked across the marble floor to the receptionist's desk, and said she was there to meet Mr. Henley for a 1:00 interview. The receptionist called Mr. Henley and asked Teresa to take a seat. When Mr. Henley arrived, they silently walked back to his office and he motioned for Teresa to sit down on the other side of a large cherrywood desk. Teresa looked around his office. She did not notice any family pictures, but did notice several proudly framed photos of Mr. Henley playing golf and tennis. Not that it mattered, but Teresa would have preferred that there be some evidence of the importance of family in his office.

Teresa slipped off her coat and draped it across the back of her chair, then took a seat. Mr. Henley started right in with rapid-fire questions. Teresa was ready for the stern, no small talk interview. Most people would have been intimidated by the coldness of the room and of Mr. Henley, but not Teresa. She had waited too long for this opportunity. As the interview progressed Teresa could feel she was breaking the ice around Mr. Henley. He especially liked her creative ideas on how to improve employee morale, and her budgeting experience. She felt that she answered all his questions perfectly, and that the job was all but served to her on a platter. Mr. Henley seemed to be impressed with her, and even grinned at some of the more light-hearted parts of their conversation.

At the end of the interview Mr. Henley informed Teresa that he was impressed with her experience, but that he would need to take time to think about his decision. Teresa thanked him and got up to leave. As she reached for her coat she noticed familiar clumps of golden hair all over the backside of her pantsuit. There were also clumps of hair in the seat where she had been sitting. Teresa's heart sank. Oh no, Max must have laid on her coat where she found it in the floor earlier. Teresa hoped that Mr. Henley would not notice as she put on her coat, but she would not be so lucky. Mr. Henley cleared his throat and handed her a lint brush. Red faced, she took the brush and cleaned the dog hair from his chair. She tried to make light of the situation, telling Mr. Henley about her awesome, yet shedful dog Max. She handed him back the lint roller, shook his hand and as professionally as she could, thanked him for the interview and walked out of his office.

When Teresa got back to her car, she called Carl and told him that she probably would not get the job. Carl was disappointed for her, but like a great husband, cheered her up by promising dinner at her favorite restaurant, *Jose Jalapeños*.

The next few days went on as normal. Carl and the kids would head out to their perspective places in the morning, with Teresa and Max at home on the continued job search. Then around 10:00am on Tuesday, Teresa got a phone call. It was Mr. Henley. "Teresa, I wanted to give you a call and invite you to join our company. I think anyone that can handle the dog hair situation with grace like you did could handle other tough issues. Besides, I liked your ideas. When can you start?"

That night for dinner Teresa fixed a celebration feast. It was complete with dessert, and included a big bone for Max!

~~~~~~~~~~~~~~~~~~~~~~~~~~~~~~~~~~~~~~~~~~~~~

"Outside of a dog, a book is man's best friend. Inside of a
dog it's too dark to read."
~ Groucho Marx

"Life should come with a trapdoor. Just a little exit hatch you
could disappear through when you'd utterly and completely
mortified yourself."
~ Michele Jaffe

# FANCY!

Marge was very good at keeping her annual well-women check-ups. She never liked them, and was always a little anxious about them until the card came in the mail telling her that everything was okay. Marge was getting up in years, having just celebrated her 69th birthday. That was how old her mother had been when she had passed away from cervical cancer, and Marge lived with that cloud hanging over her head. But she kept her worries inside, and nobody had the slightest idea that her stomach was in such knots on appointment day.

She had spent the night with her daughter while her house was having some remodeling work done. Her daughter was so sweet and thoughtful, having Marge stay until the carpenters were done. The job was to take two weeks. Marge was pleased to spend time with her daughter and family. Two weeks was long enough to get in a very good visit, but not so long that she would become a burden.

Marge made a wonderful breakfast for everyone the day of her well-women appointment. This was a *thank you* for letting her stay a couple of weeks, and a way to work off the excess nervous energy. Western omelets, sliced strawberries, bacon, and orange juice were waiting on the table for Marge's daughter, son-in-law and precious granddaughter when they got up. Everyone enjoyed a tasty meal before heading off to work or school. Marge had even given the dog, Bentley, a few scraps of leftover bacon.

After everyone had left, and Marge was alone in the house, she showered and got dressed. Marge did not want to be embarrassed at the doctor's office, so she quickly sprayed a little feminine deodorant spray in her private areas, grabbed her keys and purse, and made the short drive to the doctor's office.

The employees at the front desk knew Marge by name, for she had been coming to the same medical group for years. When they moved their practice to a different location in town, Marge was one of the local patients that followed them. She had even brought them cookies last Christmas, just to say thanks for being such a good group. Marge knew the drill. She signed in, gave the familiar faces behind the front desk a friendly smile, and took her place in the large waiting room. After ten minutes Marge heard them call her back to her exam room.

The nurse came in and took Marge's vitals, then asked her to dress in the ever-so-fashionable medical gown, then left the room. Marge quickly got undressed, put on the gown, and nervously waited on the doctor. All the time she was thinking, "They can put a man on the moon, but women still have to suffer this embarrassment every year. I bet if men had to do this they would come up with a better way."

When the doctor entered the room, he gave her the customary, "Could you slide down toward the end of the table a little bit more please." Marge did not think he really meant it. She was already hanging off the table. Marge thought he said this just as a habit. When the doctor took a seat at the end of the table he put on gloves, covered them with slimy goo, and cleared his throat. When he finally looked up in Marge's direction he said, "Fancy!" He then completed the exam, chatted with Marge a little about any medical concerns she had, and then pleasantly said good-bye.

Marge drove back to her daughter's house. When everyone got home Marge once again had a wonderful meal prepared. This time she had cooked her signature pot roast. After dinner Marge and her daughter cleaned up the table and put the dishes in the dishwasher. While they cleaned the kitchen Marge mentioned to her daughter that she thought she might change doctors. When her daughter asked why, Marge told her about the doctor saying "Fancy!" This made her very uncomfortable. Her daughter tried to figure out what the doctor meant by saying, "Fancy!" and asked her mom if she had done anything different this morning. She told her daughter that she had taken a shower, sprayed with the feminine deodorant spray in the cabinet, and then left for the doctor's.

Her daughter said, "Mom, I do not have any feminine deodorant spray. Can you show me what you used?" Marge went to the bathroom to get the spray out of the cabinet. There was a very loud "Oh, my! Oh, my!" coming from the bathroom. Marge read the label—sparkling pink hair spray, complete with glitter. Yes, doctors do see the strangest things!

~~~~~~~~~~~~~~~~~~~~~~~~~~~~~~~~~~~~~~~~~~~~~~~~

"Clear up any misunderstanding before it gets to that point"
~ Joel Miller

"Strange actions from others are generally seen through foggy glasses."
~ Joy Dye

# A REAPER IN SHEEP'S CLOTHING

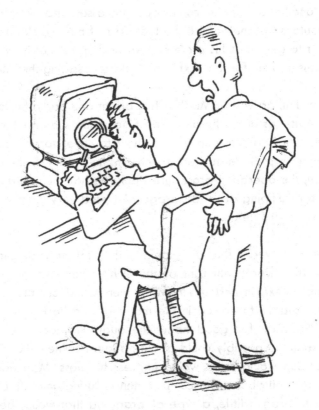

# "Is this your idea of a computer probe?"

Matt was Manager of IT for *MAO Technologies*. He loved his job, and was good at it. He had been with the company for 20 years, working his way up the salary scale. He knew that his salary was a little above market, and that worried him sometimes, but he did not let it get to him for long. He did a great job and was dedicated. *MAO Technologies* seemed to appreciate him, and he was very valuable. He knew things about how the department ran and how their data was stored that no one else did.

Mr. Mentis, Matt's boss, informed Matt that they were going to have a professional audit of the company's processes and practices. The auditor would be at their office the first part of next week. Mr. Mentis asked Matt to get all of his projects wrapped up so that he would be able to focus his time for the next two weeks on assisting the auditor.

The auditor, Jim, arrived at Matt's office bright and early the following Monday. Matt was naturally on his best behavior, showing Jim all the clever ideas he had come up with on how to save storage space on their computer system. Matt shared with Jim the details of the code he had written, the operating procedure books he had authored, and his short cuts for dumping data to storage. Jim paid very close attention, writing down every detail.

During the two weeks that Jim spent with Matt they developed a friendship. They were both fans of the *Denver Rockies*, and loved to eat at *Pete's Mexican Restaurant*. Matt even found out that Jim had to set three alarms to get up in the morning, and had a pet poodle named Spike. Matt felt good about the audit. He had given Jim all the information he possibly could about his job. He knew that the final report that Jim would write would impress his boss. Matt had been able to brag a bit about his accomplishments. During an audit a person is allowed to brag a little, a type of bragging that would be out of place in a normal conversation.

On the final Friday of Jim's audit, he did not show at the office. Matt though that a little odd. They were to have their close-out meeting with Matt's boss that morning at 9:00. Mr. Mentis told Matt that he would still like to meet with him at 9:00, just to go over how Matt thought the audit went.

At 9:00 Matt made his way to the conference room to see Mr. Mentis. As he walked into the conference room he saw Mr. Mentis, as expected. He was surprised to also see Mindy, their HR Manager. Mr. Mentis said, "Matt, please have a seat. This is not going to be easy." Matt sat down in complete confusion. Mr. Mentis informed Matt that MAO *Technologies* had to make some cuts. Matt's position was going to be redefined, and that Matt would not be part of the new IT Department. Today was Matt's last day with the company.

Sickened, Matt made his way back to his office to collect his things, with Mindy walking beside him. It became very clear to Matt that the "audit" had been a farce. Mr. Mentis just needed a way to replace Matt without disruption to their computer system. Jim would be taking Matt's place. Matt felt betrayed by Mr. Mentis and Mindy, but most of all, he felt betrayed by his new friend, Jim.

~~~~~~~~~~~~~~~~~~~~~~~~~~~~~~~~~~~~~~~~~~

It can be liberating to get fired because you realize the world doesn't end. There are other ways to make money, better jobs.
~ Ron Livingston

Getting fired is nature's way to telling you that you had the wrong job in the first place.
~ Hal Lancaster, in *The Wall Street Journal*

"The secret of business is to know something that nobody else knows."
~ Aristotle Onassis

# BOBBY, MAMA AND SISSY

## "Beats me having to make a decision."

*KJO Trucking* was a small company with 95 drivers, 20 office support professionals, and one office cat named Rover. Sherry was in charge of recruiting, interviewing, and hiring the truck drivers for *KJO*. She had met all types of people in her years of driver recruiting. She had hired young drivers just out of driving school, middle-aged drivers who were simply looking for a good, stable company, women who had the guts to enter a world assumed to be ruled by men, and even a retired college professor. She enjoyed her job, especially meeting new people, but most of all she enjoyed helping people find a career that was right for them.

One day Sherry had an interview scheduled with a man by the name of Bobby. Their meeting was so unique that trying to describe it would do it an injustice. So we will let them speak for themselves.

Scene 1: Sherry met Bobby in the lobby of the company office. Bobby had two women with him. The women looked like they had just stepped off the stage of one of the country music shows in Branson, Missouri. They had on long, late-1800s-style dresses, very big hair that had been teased and sprayed so high it added two feet to their heights, and a mannerism that was a cross between southern hospitality and backwoods isolation.

<u>Sherry</u>: Hello, Bobby, it is nice to meet you.

<u>Bobby</u>: Hello.

<u>The two women</u> (in unison): Howdy!

<u>Bobby</u>: This is Mama and Sissy.

<u>Mama</u>: We're here to help Bobby with his interview.

<u>Sissy</u>: Yeah. We wanna make sure this is gonna be a good place for our Bobby.

<u>Bobby</u>: Can they sit in the interview with me?

<u>Sherry</u>: Well, Bobby, this is your interview. If you feel you must have them with you then it is totally up to you.

<u>Bobby</u>: Yeah, I would like them with me. I feel much better when they are around.

Scene 2: Sherry, Bobby, Mama, and Sissy take seats around the oval table in the conference room. The room is not that spectacular, just a wooden table with six padded chairs, and a picture of the founder hanging on the wall.

**Mama:** Wow! This is a nice place. I bet they pay real good, Bobby.

**Sissy:** Yeah, Bobby!

**Sherry:** So, Bobby, your application reflects a strong safety record. You have 10 years of driving, with no accidents, no speeding tickets, and no failed roadside inspections. That is something to be proud of, and is the main reason I wanted to talk with you today.

**Bobby:** Yes ma'am. Thank you.

**Sherry:** The one thing that I noticed is that you seem to be looking for something in a company that you have not been able to find. I say this because you have had seven jobs in five years. Can you tell me what these companies did not provide that you are looking for?

**Mama:** He's lookin for someone that will treat him real good.

**Sissy:** Yeah, not like his last boss. (Sissy looks at Mama and they both giggle.)

**Sherry:** Bobby. What are YOU looking for in a job?

**Bobby:** Well, I guess it's like Mama said. I want someone that will treat me real good.

**Sherry:** What is your definition of good?

**Mama:** As long as he has a good paycheck, we can handle just about anything. He can be gone from home as much as you want him to be, as long as his pay is real good.

**Sherry:** Bobby, what is YOUR definition of good?

**Bobby:** Well, I can be gone as long as you want me to be, as long as my paycheck is a big 'un.

<u>Sherry</u>: Bobby, can you share with me why you left your last employment?

<u>Mama</u>: We left 'cause his boss was a jerk.

<u>Sissy</u>: Yeah, when we went to pick our Bobby up his boss was just leaving the parking lot. Me and Mama threw rocks at his car.

<u>Sherry</u>: Okay, Bobby, thank you for your time. We will be in touch.

~~~~~~~~~~~~~~~~~~~~~~~~~~~~~~~~~~~~~~~~~~~~~~

"Management is efficiency in climbing the ladder of success;
leadership determines whether the ladder is leaning against
the right wall."
~ Stephen R. Covey,

"There is no vaccine against stupidity"
~ Albert Einstein

# SMILES AT THE CREDIT UNION

# "The students asked me to lighten up."

Robin had a full-time job, four young children, and an adoring husband. She worked very hard at keeping everything at her house, her office, and in her marriage running smoothly. As hard as she worked at it, the laundry was never completely done, dishes could always be found in the dishwasher, and the volunteering events on her calendar seemed endless. She found her sanctuary in grocery shopping. This was the one time her husband took over watching the children, and she could be by herself for a little while. It was amazing how long she could make a grocery-shopping trip last, even with a list.

A few years ago, their two-year-old daughter Rachel, had contracted an unknown illness, and she had spent an entire week at *Children's Hospital*. One full week of nights spent sleeping in the recliner next to her daughter's hospital bed was a week that would stay with Robin for the rest of her life. The cries of the children would echo down the hallway. Rachel's little roommate, Susie, had just been diagnosed with leukemia. The thing that surprised Robin the most was how many of these children were in the hospital all alone. Where were their parents? Robin had reasoned with herself that the parents had other children to care for, or maybe they lived too far away to be able to stay with their sick child. Whatever the reason, Robin felt compelled to care for each and every child on Rachel's floor. These young souls had seen more pain, had cried more tears, and wanted for their mommies and daddies more than enough to last their lifetimes, and for some those lifetimes would not go on very much longer.

It took one week of tests, blood draws, and prayers before learning that Rachel had Lyme's Disease. This is a serious illness, with a simple treatment of antibiotics. Robin and her husband felt a wave of calm and answered prayers when the doctors finally told them Rachel was healthy enough to go home.

After Rachel was released from the hospital, and Robin's family routine got back to normal, Robin kept thinking about the children who were still in the hospital. The memory of their cries bouncing off the walls, and of their sad little lonely faces launched Robin into taking action. She decided to take clown classes and learn how to bring laughter back to the little faces in the hospital.

She took on the alternate ego of "BonBon." BonBon learned how to make animal balloons, perform magic tricks, and pull laughter out of their little bodies. BonBon's favorite trick was to tell the child that she was going to draw their blood. This happened to the young patients all the time, so they were very familiar with the equipment needed. BonBon would pull a tourniquet out of her pocket and loosely wrap it around their little arm. Then BonBon would quickly pull out a red crayon and scratch pad, make a few red squiggles on the paper and say, "There, I drew your blood." It never failed to bring a smile to the child's face!

One day BonBon was on her way home from a performance at *Children's Hospital*, still in costume, complete with red wig, painted face, and white lab coat with the nametag "IYQ". She suddenly remembered she needed to transfer some money from their savings to their checking account, to pay for some of the hospital bills. She was thankful that her little Rachel was back home, healthy as ever, and was happy to be paying hospital invoices instead of pharmacy bills.

BonBon pulled into the credit union parking lot. Not thinking, she got out of the car, walked up to the credit union door, opened it, and stepped inside. Suddenly the two ladies behind the counter hit the floor. BonBon realized she was still in clown attire, and started to laugh. This caused the ladies to peek over the counter at her. BonBon knew the ladies and said "Kerri, Joyce, it's me, Robin Cartrite. I've just come from performing at the hospital." With that the ladies were relieved and started laughing also. Robin walked up to the counter, made the needed money transfer, and started to leave the credit union. Just then she heard the sound of sirens. Joyce said, "Well, you probably want to get out of here before the police come. I hit the alarm button when I hit the floor. We will explain to the cops what happened." BonBon became *GoneGone* and slipped out of the door.

~~~~~~~~~~~~~~~~~~~~~~~~~~~~~~~~~~~~~~~~~~~~~~~~~

"A day without laughter is a day wasted."
~ Charlie Chaplin

"If we couldn't laugh we would all go insane."
~ Robert Frost

# INTERVIEWS WORTH HUMMMMING ABOUT

Hummm 1:
The interviewee mentioned that he was on house arrest, but had decided that coming to the interview was worth the risk.

Hummm 2:
When asked to talk about her greatest accomplishment, the interviewee said she had started her own company while she was working full time. The interviewer said, "That must have been challenging to get a company off the ground in the evenings and on weekends." The interviewee said "Oh no, I didn't build it on my own time. I did this while I was at work."

Hummm 3:
An interviewee said "I have already accepted a job with another company but, I decided to come interview with you because I thought you could use the practice."

Hummm 4:
When asked at an otherwise strong interview if he had any more questions, an interviewee replied, "Yes. I am planning on spending three months this summer hiking through Alaska. That won't be a problem, will it?"

Hummm 5:
When the interviewee was asked if she had any questions, she said, "If you hire me, how much of a warning do I get before I have to take a drug test?"

Hummm 6:
An interviewee volunteers that she is an alcoholic. It is part of her treatment that she tell everyone she meets that she is struggling with this addiction.

# JOB APPLICATIONS WORTH HUMMMMING ABOUT

Hummm 1:
The candidate gave the title of his last job on a farm as a hired hand as a "hard hand".

Hummm 2:
The candidate gave the title of his last job as a stocker at a department store as a "stoker".

Hummm 3:
The work history of a professional truck driver by the name of Tony Match included hauling fuel for a gas company.

Hummm 4:
In a cover letter a lady advised that some people think she is opinionated.

Hummm 5:
On the application, when it asked the candidate to list any criminal convictions, he wrote, "I haven't had any Mr. Meaners.

Share Your Stories:

If you enjoyed the stories in this book and would like to contribute to the next edition, simply email your story to HangInThereDay@kc.rr.com.

Please note that it will be necessary for us to change the names, locations and company of your story, to keep from embarrassing anyone. We may also add some color to your story for ease and entertainment of reading. If you submit a story and we would like to use it in a future edition, we will be in contact with you about how to recognize you in our contributions section. All stories become the property of "And you think your job stinks."

Hang in there!